TEN OLD PAILS

written by
Nicholas Heller

pictures by
Yossi Abolafia

GREENWILLOW BOOKS, NEW YORK

FOR AMBER

—N. H.

FOR YOAV

—Y. A.

Watercolor paints and a black pen were used for the full-color art.
The text type is Schneidler.

Text copyright © 1994 by Nicholas Heller
Illustrations copyright © 1994 by Yossi Abolafia
Printed in Singapore by Tien Wah Press
First Edition   10 9 8 7 6 5 4 3 2 1

Library of Congress Cataloging-in-Publication Data
Heller, Nicholas.
Ten old pails / by Nicholas Heller; illustrated by Yossi Abolafia,
        p.   cm.
Summary: A boy tells how he got each of ten pails and what he
is going to do with them.
ISBN 0-688-12419-4 (trade).   ISBN 0-688-12420-8 (lib. bdg.)
[1. Play—Fiction.   2. Pails—Fiction.]   I. Abolafia, Yossi, ill.   II. Title.
III. Title: 10 old pails.   PZ7. H37426Te   1994
[E]—dc20   92-31511   CIP   AC

I have ten old pails, and I'll tell you where they came from.

The first was a milk pail,

until an angry cow gave it a kick
and a great big dent.

The second used to be a water pail,

but when it got old it started to leak.

The third was for carrying coal to the stove,
but that was a long time ago,
and we don't use coal anymore.

The fourth was the dinner pail for our pigs,
but when the pigs had piglets,
they needed a bigger pail.

The fifth pail was the kitchen garbage pail,
but the top was missing,

and it wasn't very nice.
So one day we bought a new one.

The sixth pail used to be full of sand.
We kept it in the barn,
just in case there was a fire,

until my father said,
"This will work much better."

I found the seventh pail in the cellar,
all full of golf balls.
Where did they come from? I don't know....

None of us plays golf,
so I gave them to my uncle.

In the spring we hang pails from maple trees
to collect the sap for syrup,
but the handle broke on this one,
and now it's my eighth pail.

The ninth one I found
when we went to the beach.
Someone lost it, I guess.

The tenth pail is really an empty paint can.
I said, "Wait! Don't throw that away, please,"

because I needed one more pail.
And now I'll tell you why.

I need two for my feet,
and one for my head,

and three for my
rocket-pack in back.

This one is for food and water.   That one is for moon rocks.

The big one is my launch pad.

And the last one I will leave for my mother!